St. Patrick
and the
Three Brave Mice

St. Patrick
and the
Three Brave Mice

By Joyce A. Stengel

Illustrated by Herb Leonhard

PELICAN PUBLISHING COMPANY
GRETNA 2009

For Alice and Peter, with love—J. S.

*The word "Pelican" and the depiction of a pelican are trademarks
of Pelican Publishing Company, Inc., and are registered in the
U.S. Patent and Trademark Office.*

Library of Congress Cataloging-in-Publication Data

Stengel, Joyce A.
  St. Patrick and the three brave mice / Joyce A. Stengel.
      p. cm.
  Summary: When St. Patrick has driven all but one crafty snake out of Ireland, the mice—Ryan, Brian, and Tulla—devise a risky plan of their own to outwit the wily reptile.
  ISBN 978-1-58980-663-4 (hardcover : alk. paper) [1. Mice—Fiction. 2. Snakes—Fiction. 3. Courage—Fiction. 4. Patrick, Saint, 373?-463?—Fiction. 5. Ireland—History—To 1172—Fiction.] I. Title. II. Title: Saint Patrick and the three brave mice.
  PZ7.S82885St 2009
  [E]—dc22

                              2008035591

Printed in Singapore
Published by Pelican Publishing Company, Inc.
1000 Burmaster Street, Gretna, Louisiana 70053

St. Patrick and the Three Brave Mice

Many years ago, St. Patrick traveled the roads and byways of Ireland driving out the snakes with a bell.

But one crafty, clever snake escaped. This snake slithered through meadow and forest, day and night, hunting for tasty mouse meals.

One night, three little mice, Ryan, Brian, and Tulla, cuddled in their nest. Ryan and Brian soon fell asleep. But Tulla was restless.

When the moon rose high, she scrambled
from the nest. Light as a whisper, she skittered
up her favorite hill. She snuggled into a leaf
and gazed up at the stars and the moon,
listening to the night's sounds.

She heard a loud snore. *Zzzzzzzzzzzzzz.*
She looked down the hill. There, under a
tree, a man slept. A bell glowed at
his side.

Tulla's whiskers twitched.
Could it be St. Patrick and
his miraculous bell?

Then Snake slithered from the forest.
Tulla hid behind a mushroom and peeked out.

Snake seized a mouthful of grass. He inched
his way to the bell and poked the grass around
the clapper. Time and again, he stuffed grass
into the bell.

When he had finished, that crafty, clever Snake slid his tail through the bell's handle and stole it away.

Tulla had to save the bell! She scurried after Snake, following him to his lair.

Snake coiled around the bell and sleepily closed his eyes. His forked tongue darted in and out. Was he dreaming of mouse meat?

Tulla darted back to the nest.

"Wake up!" she cried. "Snake stole St. Patrick's bell."

"You had a nightmare," Ryan said.

"'Tis your imagination," Brian said.

"You're daft," they said together.

"No! Get up," Tulla insisted. "I have a plan."

Grumbling, Ryan and Brian followed Tulla to the hill. They looked down and there was St. Patrick, snoring under the tree. But no bell.

Tulla led them to Snake's lair and whispered her plan. The three mice scattered and gathered strong grasses. They braided a rope.

"Now, one of us must tie this rope to the
bell's handle," Tulla told them.

"You are the smallest," Ryan said.

"And the lightest," Brian said.

"And the quietest," they said together.

Trembling, Tulla grabbed the rope with her teeth and dragged it towards the bell. Just as she was about to loop the end of the rope through the bell's handle, Snake's tongue darted out. Tulla didn't move. Not a whisker.

Snake settled back to sleep and Tulla tied the rope. The three mice tugged the bell back to St. Patrick.

Blade by blade they removed the grass. Tulla
was about to snatch the very last blade when Brian
squeaked, "Snake is coming!"

Quick as a wink, Tulla clutched the bell's
clapper. "Stand the bell up!" she cried.
Snake slithered closer.
Ryan and Brian pushed the bell upright.
Snake hissed and reared his head.

Tulla swung on the clapper.
Bong!

St. Patrick sprang to his feet. Tulla scampered out as he snatched up the bell.

Then St. Patrick rang his bell
—*BONG! BONG! BONG!*—
and drove that crafty, clever Snake
to the sea.

"Hip, hip, hurray!" Ryan, Brian, and Tulla cheered as Snake slithered into the water and disappeared from Ireland forever.

And that is the tale of the three brave mice who helped St. Patrick drive the last snake from Ireland.